The
Minstrel Knight

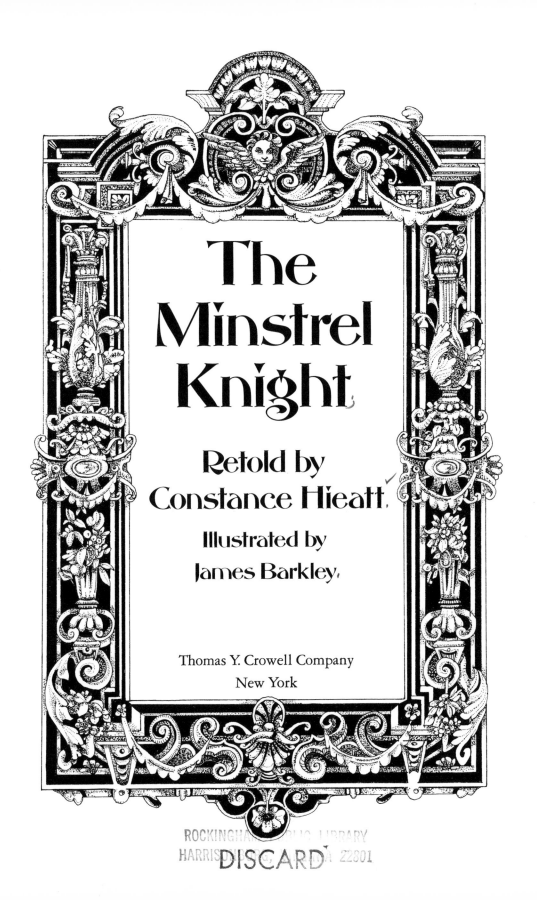

The Minstrel Knight

Retold by
Constance Hieatt

Illustrated by
James Barkley

Thomas Y. Crowell Company
New York

ROCKINGHAM PUBLIC LIBRARY
HARRISONBURG, VIRGINIA 22801
DISCARD

J398.2
H

Retold by Constance Hieatt

THE CASTLE OF LADIES
THE JOY OF THE COURT
THE KNIGHT OF THE CART
THE KNIGHT OF THE LION
THE MINSTREL KNIGHT
SIR GAWAIN AND THE GREEN KNIGHT
THE SWORD AND THE GRAIL

Copyright © 1974 by Constance Hieatt
Illustrations copyright © 1974 by James Barkley
All rights reserved. Except for use in a review,
the reproduction or utilization of this work in
any form or by any electronic, mechanical, or
other means, now known or hereafter invented,
including xerography, photocopying, and record-
ing, and in any information storage and retrieval
system is forbidden without the written permission
of the publisher. Published simultaneously in
Canada by Fitzhenry & Whiteside Limited, Toronto.

Designed by Angela Foote

Manufactured in the United States of America

Library of Congress Cataloging in Publication Data
Hieatt, Constance B The minstrel knight.
SUMMARY: Sir Orfeo's kingdom is a happy one until
the King of the Fairies takes away his bride.
Bibliography: p. [1. Fairy tales]
I. Barkley, James, illus. II. Title.
PZ8.H53Mi3 [Fic] 73-9556 ISBN 0-690-00210-6

1 2 3 4 5 6 7 8 9 10

For Carolyn and Melissa

Contents

Preface

A reader of the stories of King Arthur and his court knows that their world is not exactly like our own. In these tales, people may become invisible, ugly things can become beautiful, and ordinary objects (or people) may possess extraordinary powers. Such elements of magic and the marvelous are one of the reasons we enjoy such stories. We ourselves are limited and confined by time, space, and the "laws of nature," but the Arthurian world is freer. We can sometimes see more there of the true nature of our world simply because some of the arbitrary limits have been removed.

Arthurian stories resemble what we call "fairy

tales'' in this respect, and for good reason. Both draw on the same traditions of an otherworldly people known as Faerie. But the tales of King Arthur often preserve much earlier—and more interesting—ideas of these strange people than those we find in simpler, shorter folk tales. Thus, Arthur's sister Morgan le Fay, whose name means ''Morgan the Fairy,'' sometimes seems wonderfully beautiful and sometimes hideously ugly; sometimes a tremendous help to men and sometimes a dangerous enemy; but always the possessor of marvelous powers, unavailable to ordinary human beings. This is because she is a fairy: her nature is not human and she cannot be expected to act as a mere human would.

The Minstrel Knight comes from the tradition which gives us so odd a figure as Morgan. The stories on which I have drawn tell of an Other World, which exists side by side with the world of men but is not the same. It may be close at hand, but it is separate, often almost impossible to find. The people of this world of Faerie are not quite like the ''Good'' and ''Bad'' fairies of the folktales because they are both good and bad at once—or neither, depending on the point of view. The same group may appear to be beautiful and charming, like the dazzling court of my fairy monarch Midir, or terrible and threatening, as is my Wild Hunt. Nor are the reasons for their changeable behavior always clear to men. When my hero, Orfeo, breaks a branch from a tree he does so with the most innocent of motives, but he unwittingly breaks a rule known only to the people of Faerie, and he must pay the consequences. That is the danger when the two worlds come in contact, for man has no way of knowing the rules of that Other World.

That world does, however, abide by rules, just as man's world does, and those who are wise enough to observe these rules may be amply rewarded. Orfeo's story concerns the working of rules in both worlds. Such rules resemble music in that if you put the right notes together the result is harmonious and pleasing, while a wrong note can spoil the whole effect. That is one good reason why Sir Orfeo is a musician.

Harping in the Halls
of Camelot

hen King Arthur held court at Camelot, everyone in the world longed to visit that famous castle, and sooner or later, many people did. Among those who were drawn by the fame of the king and his queen, Guinevere, and the bold knights and lovely ladies who bore them company, there were always many minstrels. Harpers came to sing their songs and play their music for the pleasure of the court, and then departed to sing songs of Camelot in distant lands. Nor did the court itself lack musicians, for there was no man there, from such famous knights as Sir Gawain down to the youngest squire, who could not tune a harp and delight the company with song.

Thus no one thought it strange when one winter evening a knight came to Camelot with a harp slung over his shoulder, as well as a shield that had seen many battles. The folk of the court welcomed the stranger and helped him to remove his armor. Then they led him to a place at the table, where he could rest after his journey and refresh himself with food and drink.

As a splendid meal was served and eaten, the ladies of the court smiled at the handsome stranger—a tall man, with fine dark eyes. He responded gravely to their greetings, and when the knights asked him about his journey, they, too, found that while the strange knight answered courteously, he seemed to be a very quiet man. Perhaps this was because he wished to listen rather than to talk. The music of the king's pipers, sometimes merry and lively and sometimes sweetly sad, seemed to hold a special interest for him.

After the board was cleared that night, a minstrel stepped forward and sat at the king's feet. Softly playing on his harp, he sang of a hero who had conquered a terrible dragon. No one listened more carefully than the strange knight, and when the minstrel had finished everyone still sat in silence for a while as the last notes of the harp hung in the air. Then the stranger suddenly said, "There are other songs about the same hero. Will you sing us another one, minstrel?"

"Alas, sir," said the minstrel, "that is all I know. Will you take my harp, and teach us one of those songs?"

"Gladly," said the knight, and he picked up the harp and ran his fingers gently over the strings. When he had tuned it to his satisfaction, he started to sing in a fine, clear voice. He sang of the young hero who crossed the water to battle a hideous monster-woman, and of the marvelous sword with which he laid her grim spirit to rest. It was a very long ballad, but it did not seem so to those who listened: never in their lives had they heard such singing. Even though the most famous minstrels in the world came to Camelot, the music of the minstrel knight made everyone feel as if he had never heard true harmony before.

When he had finished his song, the hour was late, and it was time for bed. But before the company parted for the night, King Arthur said to his guest, "Sir knight—sir harper—we would be glad to know who you are, if you wish to tell us; but whoever you may be, you are most welcome here. We hope you will linger with us, so that we may hear more of your music."

The minstrel knight bowed to the king, as he returned the harp to its owner. "I will be pleased to stay for a while, lord," he said, "for it is a bitter time of the year for traveling, and my country is far away. My name is Orfeo, and my home, the land called Tracience, is many days' journey from here, beyond deep rivers and high mountains."

Thus it happened that all through the rest of that winter, while the snows lay deep around King Arthur's castle, the halls of Camelot often rang with the marvelous songs of Sir Orfeo. Whenever he tuned his harp, knights and ladies gathered around him. Cooks tiptoed up the kitchen stairs and grooms came in from the stables to listen. Children left their play, and even the babies in their cradles ceased their cries and smiled at his songs. He sang of wars and kingdoms lost or won, of feuds and monsters and heroes young and old; he sang of spring and the joys and sorrows of lovers, of saints and miracles, and of strange lands far away. Sometimes he made everyone laugh with tales of fools and clowns, and sometimes he made them weep with pity or fear. Then one night a young page, sitting close to Sir Orfeo's side, said, "But tell us, sir, Are your stories true?"

"All good tales tell of things that are true," Sir Orfeo replied.

"That may be," said the boy, "but have you seen these deeds with your own eyes?"

"Some, I have seen indeed," said Sir Orfeo.

"And some I have learned from others, as we all must do."

"Then tell us," urged the page, "a tale that really happened—something you saw yourself. Good Sir Orfeo, sing to us of your own adventures!"

"Well, then," said Sir Orfeo, "I shall sing of the Fair One of the Forest."

And he struck up a tune on his harp which was more moving than any they had heard before. Strange and lovely, it was like no other song on earth. This is the tale he sang to them.

A knight was roaming beyond the borders of his native land one day, riding through a mighty forest, deep and dark. All was so still and hushed there that it was like a dream land. The branches of the trees scarcely whispered as they moved in the breeze, and even the calls of the birds were muted and muffled, so deep was the hush in the heart of that wood. Sometimes the knight thought he heard sounds as if a foot rustled the leaves somewhere nearby in the shade of the towering trees, but when he turned to look for the source of the noise, nothing moved at all, and the silence was deeper than ever.

Uneasy, he thought that this was no place for a human being—there was no sign that any other had ever come this way. At last he felt that he would have to turn back the silence, somehow, and he reached for his harp and began to play a tune as he rode along, singing softly to himself. As he did so, the air seemed to freshen and grow less oppressive. His heart grew light, and he sang out more merrily. Now, as he rode on his way, touching his harp and singing, the forest came to life; small furry beasts appeared on the ground around him, and birds flew over his head as if they wished to listen to his song.

And then he felt that the very trees were moving around him. Now he reached a grove where the sun shone through the leaves, casting intricate patterns on the ground below. He stopped, tethered his horse, and sat down to watch the forest life as he sang in the heart of the wood. And when he began to sing again, the trees and shrubs seemed to draw close to him. He played and watched for some time, and gradually he saw that these were not trees at all, but maidens— young girls as slender as saplings, dressed in gowns of brown and silvery-gray. They were crowned with wild, leafy garlands, so that until they drew near they could not be seen among the surrounding trees. But now they came forward to be closer to his strains, and he could see them clearly.

The lady who led the group was the loveliest he had ever seen. Her beautiful face and soft, fair hair, falling in vinelike tendrils over her curved shoulders, were crowned with a wreath woven of sprigs of golden berries.

As he gazed at the lady's violet eyes, he found he

was singing to her alone, making a new song about how her beauty turned his heart within him. Then the evening shadows grew deep, and the knight let his song fade away. As soon as he put his harp aside, the forest maidens fled, and vanished into the wood; birds and beasts alike retreated into the depths of the forest, and he was quite alone again.

He spent the night on a mossy bank, pondering over the strangeness of the forest and the loveliness of the fair maiden crowned with golden berries. By the time morning came, he knew there was nothing he wished for so much as another sight of the fair one of the woodland. And so he stayed for an enchanted season in the forest, singing to the maidens of the wood, who appeared whenever he sang, until at last a day came when the lady of the golden wreath spoke to him, and shyly asked if he would teach her to play the harp. In the end, the forest rang with life and merriment, as the knight and his fair forest lady made music together, and all the other maidens danced for joy around them.

There Sir Orfeo ended his song. But the young page beside him said, "I should like to see that lady. Where is the forest where you found her?"

"It is a long, weary way," said Sir Orfeo, "beyond the snow-topped mountains. But even if you were to make your way there, you would not find my fair one, for she is now my wife and dwells in my own halls. There she is known as the lady Etain.''

''Does she miss the forest?'' asked the page.

''You would have to ask that question of her,'' said Orfeo with a smile, ''but I do not think so. She plays in the gardens as merrily as a kitten, and she sings like a skylark as she rests in the shade at noon. There is no one more loved than she in all our land.''

Now the torches were burning low, and Sir Orfeo put aside his harp. The king rose, and everyone was about to retire when suddenly a squire entered the hall in great haste and called the minstrel knight aside. ''Sir Orfeo,'' he said, ''a knight has just arrived who wishes to speak to you at once, though the hour is late. He says that he brings news of your land and an urgent message from your lady, Etain.''

''I pray no ill fortune has befallen her,'' said Orfeo in alarm, and he followed the squire out of the room at once.

Tidings of Discord

s Sir Orfeo entered the chamber to which the squire led him, the messenger jumped to his feet and greeted him joyfully. "My good friend Amilon!" said Orfeo, for this was a knight who had been in his family's service for many years. "It warms my heart to see you. But what brings you here? Tell me your tidings, my friend."

Sir Amilon's face fell and he said, "Alas, my lord, I have ridden night and day to bring you this news, yet now I find it hard to know how to begin."

"Has something befallen my lady Etain?" asked Sir Orfeo.

"Yes, my lord," said Amilon, "but calm yourself: she is well, and sends you her loving greetings."

"What is it, then? Tell me at once, sir," said Orfeo with a stern face.

"My lady bids you come home in all haste," replied Sir Amilon. "She is suffering great unkindness at the hands of Ganlin, your steward; and so, to tell the truth, is all your land. In his greed for gold he has robbed both rich and poor. Any who are bold enough to protest soon find themselves in prison. His rule has been harsh and unjust, and he cares for no man's rights. When I protested his treatment of the lady Etain, who is now a prisoner and can do nothing to help your people, he would have thrown me in prison myself. No doubt he would have taken my life—as he has those of others—but I fought my way out of the castle and fled, pursued by soldiers in Ganlin's pay."

"This is most terrible news," said Sir Orfeo. "Ganlin has been my trusted steward for many long years now, and I thought him the one man to rule my land in my absence. If he is proved unfaithful, what man in the world can I trust?"

"You may trust me, my lord," said Amilon quietly. "But if you doubt my word, pray read this letter from your wife; you can see that it is in her own hand."

He held forth a sealed message. Sir Orfeo gazed at the seal, which he recognized at once; then he tore the letter open. For several moments he stood there in silence, reading and rereading the letter. At last he sighed, as he put it down. "Yes," he said, "that is my lady's hand, and she bids me come at once. She says I may trust you to tell me the true state of affairs. I have no choice but to believe the terrible news you bring me. Will you be ready to travel with me at break of day tomorrow?"

"I am ready now, sir," said the faithful Amilon.

"No, my good Amilon," said Sir Orfeo. "You must have a few hours rest, at least, although my heart yearns to depart without delay."

Sir Amilon knew that his lord was right, and so the two men parted for a few hours. The time was all too short, for Amilon was so weary he could have slept for a week and Orfeo was ill prepared for the news he had just received. He had as yet made no preparations for the long trip home. Yet long before the sun had fully risen over the horizon on that bleak March day, both men were an hour or two's ride away from Camelot. There had been no time for them to take leave of King Arthur, or to explain the need which drove them, and there was no one left behind to make their apologies to the court, except for the squire who had received Sir Amilon the night before. He could only assure the king that a most terrible necessity had driven his guest to leave so suddenly.

The two men spurred on their horses—and themselves—without mercy, halting only when they could go no farther, and then only long enough to fetch their breaths and draw strength for the next lap of the journey. Though the weather was bitterly cold, they spent no night under a roof and ate no real meal until they were at the borders of the realm called Tracience, the land of Sir Orfeo. When they had at last reached the great forest which ringed their country, they searched for a woodman's cottage, thinking that there they might find shelter for the night—and food, however plain and humble. Most of all, they hoped for fresh news of the kingdom before they set foot in the castle precincts.

But it was not as easy as it should have been. No friendly spirals of smoke rose out of the forest to point the way to a woodman's hut, and when they did by chance stumble upon a cottage, time and again they found it barred up and silent. There were no children playing around the doorstep and no comfortable housewife or hospitable host to welcome them at the gate. At last they did spy one wisp of smoke rising from a grove and made their way toward it eagerly. No palace or castle had ever looked more charming to either of them than did this simple thatched cottage surrounded by spring flowers and, even better to the eyes of the weary travelers, a flourishing kitchen garden, green with spring cabbages and the first shoots of onions and parsley. The gardener himself was

leaning on the handle of his spade, quietly watching the two knights approach. As they drew up outside his gate, he silently swung it open so that they might enter.

Then, just at that moment, the quiet of the evening air was shattered by a sudden loud horn blast in the wood nearby, and the answering calls of a thousand wild, shrill trumpets echoed from all directions. Their horses jumped and shied. The two knights were almost thrown to the ground. But the man who held the gate was not disturbed. "'Tis but hunting horns," he said in brief explanation.

"But who is hunting in this forest?" asked Sir Amilon. "Our hunters never sound the horn so wildly."

"Ah," said the woodman, "that is a question no man can answer. That is why so many of my neighbors have left the wood: those who hunt in it these days are not of our kind. But come inside, sirs, if you will, and I shall tell you of what goes on in this forest while you rest and refresh yourselves."

Orfeo and his comrade thankfully accepted this invitation. They tethered their horses in a grassy spot and made their way under the low lintel of the cottage door. While they sat comfortably by the woodman's fireside, he prepared a simple but delicious meal of hare stewed with fresh greens and potherbs. It was not until the last drop of fragrant sauce had been wiped up with coarse bread and washed down with strong cider that they returned to the subject of the hunters in the forest.

"These are strange days, my lords," the woodman told them, "for they say that the dead ride amongst us here. Those who hunt in our wood sound like a great thundering troop of riders, but there is never a blade of grass bent where they have passed, and no man has ever seen them take any game. It is said that one of them rides with a tattered rope about his neck as if he had just come down from the gallows."

"No marvel, then, that your neighbors did not relish their presence," said Amilon. "But you are not afraid of them yourself?"

"It is not for me that they ride," said the woodman, gazing into the fire. "They are come from the realm of Faerie; let the man who has offended them take heed. I know when they came, and I know when they will go."

"And when will that be?" asked Amilon, growing somewhat impatient.

"They were first heard when the steward who rules this land—may his name be cursed!—made our good lady a prisoner in her own halls. They mean no harm to any but the man who oppresses that lady. Let *him* beware! Nor will they depart unless our lord returns and frees her from this oppression. May he come soon!"

Sir Orfeo had not spoken until now. He had been sitting with his back to the light, his face shadowed by the hood of his cloak. Now he threw back the hood and said to the woodman, "He is here. What more can you tell me, woodman?"

"My lord Sir Orfeo!" cried the woodman. "Blessed is your coming!" And he fell down on his knees, weeping for joy.

Orfeo raised him, urging him to tell all he knew of the state of the realm. The news the woodman could give was not good: matters went as badly as Sir Amilon had said, and worse. "But, good lord," said the woodman, "you need have no fear. Your people will welcome your return with great rejoicing. With them behind you, there is little Ganlin can do to harm you. But I would go carefully if I were you. I think this is Sir Amilon I see by your side: there is an order out for his immediate arrest. Ganlin has promised a fine reward for him, alive or dead. There are those who would do much for Ganlin's gold."

His guests assured him they would proceed with caution. Through the night they rested and pondered, considering how best to approach the castle. From time to time they slept, but only fitfully, for sudden blasts of the wild hunting horns disturbed the peace of the forest all night long.

The True Friends
and the False

s Sir Orfeo and Sir Amilon rode out of the forest in the morning, they heard the sudden twang of a bow-string, and an arrow flashed between their heads. "Halt!" cried a rough voice to their left, and they saw a band of archers kneeling there, ready to let fly a swarm of arrows if they did not obey at once. Rather than lose their horses to the archers, they drew up and waited for the leader of the band to approach them. As a burly yeoman came toward them, Sir Orfeo said, "What is the meaning of this, archer? Have the

24

men of this land turned such ruffians that they threaten the lives of innocent travelers?"

"Not all that come from this forest are innocent, sir," said the yeoman. "And there's some as is wanted at the castle." He gazed sternly at Sir Amilon, while the rest of the band began to move toward them, weapons in hand.

"If you mean my friend here, you are right; your lord most surely has need of him," said Orfeo.

"And you, sir," said the yeoman, "should know that you are in dangerous company. You had best come with us, too." He started to raise his hand as a signal to the others to close in.

But Orfeo now threw back his cloak, so that they could see him clearly, and said, "I am your lord."

At this the men let their weapons drop, and roared out a mighty cheer as they crowded around Sir Orfeo, gladly welcoming him. "Enough, good fellows," said Orfeo. "I thank you for your welcome. Now perhaps you had better form an escort as we ride on to the castle."

Thus it was that Sir Orfeo returned to his home attended by one other knight and a troop of bowmen, who ran before him proclaiming the news of the lord's return in the streets of the town. Everywhere they passed, the folk came out of their houses and cheered lustily. The stir and commotion could not help but reach the ears of those in the castle long before the party arrived there, and when the steward, Sir Ganlin, learned that the people were welcoming back their lord and his, he came out from the halls of the castle. He awaited Sir Orfeo in the courtyard there, stepping forward to hold his stirrup as he dismounted. "Welcome home, my lord," he said, quietly.

"Thank you, Ganlin," said Orfeo. "But it is hard to believe I am home when I do not see my dear wife coming to greet me. Where is she? Is she ill, perhaps? Or has she gone out with her ladies to look for spring flowers in the hills?"

"No, my lord," said Ganlin, "she is not ill, nor has she gone out with her ladies to gather spring flowers. Would that it were so simple a matter—I think it would be best if we retired to discuss this in private," he added with a cold glance at Sir Amilon.

"Very well," said Orfeo, "but Sir Amilon will come with us."

Ganlin opened his mouth to protest, but one glance at Orfeo's stern face told him that this would be no use. After a moment, he shrugged his shoulders and turned aside, bowing in the direction of an anteroom, where the three men now went.

"Lord Orfeo," the steward began, "I must inform you that you have been nursing a nest of traitors in your home."

"Indeed," said Sir Orfeo. "Get on, man. What have you to tell me?"

"In your absence," said Ganlin, "the abandoned creature you call your wife entered into a plot with the false friend who is now by your side. Fortunately, I was able to overhear their conversation when they thought no one was near. They planned to ambush you and murder you on your return, so that they might gain control of the realm and its riches for themselves. I heard that woman Etain assure your precious Sir Amilon that she longed for the day when she would be his, and he would rule the land with her by his side."

"You wicked cur," cried Amilon, "how dare you tell such lies?"

"Be silent, Amilon," said Sir Orfeo; "I have heard your story, and now I want to hear Ganlin's. Ganlin, take me to my wife. I wish you to confront her with this tale in my presence."

"Of course, my lord," replied the steward. "I am only sorry that you cannot be spared so painful a scene."

Now Ganlin led Orfeo and Amilon into the ladies' chambers, and at last Orfeo saw his lady Etain, sitting in a corner, strumming her lyre in a mournful tune. She looked like a wilted flower.

Etain glanced up quickly as the three knights entered the room, then rose with a start when she saw her husband. She ran across the room, stretching her arms out toward him, but Ganlin stepped in front of her and grasped her by the wrist. "Do not be in so great a hurry, madame," he said. "There is much to be settled here. I have just informed my master, your husband, of how I overheard you plotting foully with this fellow Amilon. You cannot deny that the two of you planned to murder Sir Orfeo and take his riches for your own."

"Oh, my lord, do not believe this dreadful story!" cried Etain. "Never could I do such a thing. And as for Amilon, he is your faithful friend, unlike this villain here!"

"Madame," said Ganlin, still holding her wrist in a tight grasp, "you will not be able to deceive your poor husband so easily. He has known me for many years, and he knows I am honest and faithful. But how true it is that no man can trust a woman!"

"Ganlin," said Orfeo, "how can a man tell his true friends from the false?"

"Surely, lord," the steward replied, "you can put your faith in those you have learned to trust—unless they are proved unworthy."

"You are quite right about that," said Orfeo. "You should know that I trust my wife. Release her at once."

And he went to Etain, and embraced her. "Do not grieve, my love," he said. "This foolish man did not understand the harmony and confidence that is between us two, nor did he realize that I could never believe his outrageous tale. Now, sir," he added to Ganlin, "be gone from my sight. I do not ever wish to see you again."

"You cannot mean that, lord!" Ganlin protested. "Perhaps I may have misjudged the words I heard these two saying, but I have always acted with your best interests in mind, and—"

"Stop this at once, and leave my land," said Sir Orfeo.

"We shall see about that," said Ganlin, in an entirely different tone of voice. "Ho, guards! Come at once! Help, here!"

And, as the knights outside ran into the room at his call, he cried, "This is not Sir Orfeo, but a rank impostor! Do not be deceived—take him prisoner, men!"

But his ruse did not work. The men knew their lord well, and Sir Ganlin's words only proved his treachery. The guards turned on the traitor himself, but Orfeo cried out at once, "Stop, do not harm him! I will have no blood shed in my domain, not even that of a wretch like Ganlin. Carry him to the edge of the wood, and see that he leaves my land forever."

"Is that wise, sir?" protested Amilon. "He may easily come sneaking back here, determined to do you harm. For the sake of your good lady's peace of mind, put the fellow to death."

"What do you say, my dear?" Orfeo asked Etain.

ROCKINGHAM PUBLIC LIBRARY
HARRISON

Etain gazed calmly into Ganlin's face. "I wish no man ill," she said. "Let him go hence unharmed, for me."

"Go, then," said Orfeo to Ganlin, "but do not let your face be seen again in this realm, for I cannot vouch for my men's restraint." To Amilon he then added, "Go with the men as they take him away, and see that my orders are carried out."

"As you wish, sir," said Amilon, and, under his direction, the troop of men led their prisoner away, firmly, but without roughness or violence. Sir Ganlin made no further attempt to protest his innocence—that would clearly have been of no use now—but went along, without another word, glowering hideously.

The streets of the town were still full of people, discussing the return of their lord in high excitement. Their feelings about his cruel steward were quite evident. When they saw him being led out as a prisoner, a hostile silence descended on the crowd, then came a buzz of low murmuring, and an occasional jeer. At last one man raised his voice and cried, "Where are you taking him, Sir Amilon?"

"To the forest," said Amilon. "Sir Orfeo has commanded that no man is to hurt him, and he must be allowed to go free as long as he leaves our land for good."

"Hurrah!" cried two or three, though there were many who would have preferred to start throwing stones at the prisoner.

By the time the little procession reached the edge of the forest, a large crowd straggled in the rear, many of them muttering threats and armed with sticks and stones. As the knights released him, Ganlin looked back at the faces of the mob; he found nothing which tempted him to return the way he had come. Shaking his fist in a last angry gesture, he turned and ran into the wood. Then a horn rang out; and then another, and another, and so many others that the ear could not tell how many. The whole forest seemed to shiver with the din. The crowd, which had been about to break loose and rush after the hated figure of the steward, wavered and fell back. Men looked at each other with fearful faces, and many covered their ears to block out the terrible, unearthly sound.

"Go home, my friends," said Sir Amilon. "Whatever goes on in the forest, it is not our business."

The townsmen were glad enough to follow orders this time. Most of them were quick to shut their doors and bar their windows when they were safely inside, for the wild blasts resounding in the forest could be clearly heard in the heart of the town and they struck terror into everyone's heart.

A Horn Sounds
in the Wood

After a while, when the horns had reached a peak of sound that was almost unbearable to hear, they faded away again, and quiet returned to the countryside. Still, the people remained indoors that night, and for several days thereafter no one dared to venture into the forest. But when almost a week had passed since Sir Orfeo's homecoming, a group of young boys went into the woods to gather fuel. An hour later, they came out of the forest, running as fast as they could. They ran straight to the castle, seeking Sir Amilon.

When he had met with them, Amilon went to Sir Orfeo and said, "The boys of the town have strange tidings for us. They have found Ganlin's body in the forest, quite dead. He had been ridden down, it seems. There are traces of the hooves of many horses. The lads think the deed was done by the Wild Hunt."

"Are you sure that none of our people followed him in malice?" asked Orfeo. "He was much hated, it is clear; someone might have wished to make his death look like an accident or the work of strange powers."

"I am quite certain that no man followed him," said Sir Amilon. "It is most strange."

"Strange, indeed," said Orfeo. "But if the people believe that the Wild Hunt has done this, will this increase their fear of the forest?"

"Of course," said Sir Amilon. "No one wishes to set foot in the forest, since such things can happen there."

"Then you and I must try to set their fears at rest—or prove that they are right, whichever may be the case. Are you willing to walk in the forest with me?"

"I will walk wherever you lead, my lord," said Sir Amilon.

"Come, then," said Sir Orfeo. "We will go on foot through the town, so that all may see where we are bound, and find—whatever we may find in the forest."

Sir Orfeo and Sir Amilon returned from the forest

later that day with no tidings at all to be told. The woods seemed calm and quiet; no horns had disturbed the peace of the afternoon. And so matters continued. No further sign of the Wild Hunt was seen in any part of the land, and it was not long before the woodmen and their families began to move back into their forest cottages.

In other ways, too, a new peace returned to the countryside. Sir Orfeo was kept busy for many weeks straightening out the troubles which his steward had caused: many cases at law had to be heard, many injured families helped, and a few bold villains, who had thrived in the lord's absence, had to be chastised and brought to order. Before the spring had passed, however, all was once more harmonious, and nowhere more so than in the halls of the lord himself.

Sir Orfeo and his fair lady Etain set a joyful example to all that land. Neither one ever spoke a harsh word to the other—or to anyone else; and their delight in each other's company was charming to see. As word of the lord's return now spread far and wide, many harpers and minstrels were drawn to their castle, for they knew that there was always a welcome there for anyone who could play delightful music. The land rang with the sounds of harps and sweet song instead of the shrill, wild sounds of hunting horns.

Now when June came, and the fields and woods were fragrant with blossoms, Orfeo and Etain went forth to enjoy the beauty of the forest on a fine, sunny day. They took with them a merry group of knights and ladies, some of whom carried lutes and harps and well-tuned pipes. A crowd of pages and serving men followed them. The company rode along a woodland trail where the branches of the trees formed an archway over their heads, while the sun shone through onto a carpet of flowers below.

When they had found a pleasant valley, they stopped and enjoyed their midday meal sitting on the grass. Then they danced and sang and played games until, in the heat of the sun, some of the ladies began to feel very drowsy, and Etain thought that she would like to take a nap. She lay down in the shade of an enormous oak tree, and many of her ladies joined her there. But Orfeo and most of the other knights wished to ride farther into the forest, and so they left the ladies there, with a group of squires and pages to escort them back to the castle, while they rode on by themselves.

By midafternoon Sir Orfeo had strayed away from his comrades. Now he found himself in a part of the forest where he had never been before. Since there seemed to be a well-marked track, this did not worry him, and he rode straight on. As he went on his way, it suited his carefree mood to strum on the harp that he usually carried with him. He hummed a cheerful tune, then found words and sang as he rode:

I know a maiden so fair to behold
Her beauty shines brighter than silver or gold.
The worth of this treasure can scarcely be told:
Like sapphires or rubies, too rare to be sold;
As pure as a diamond, as precious as jade,
No gem is as fine as this gentle sweet maid.

Many animals frisked about him—squirrels and
hares and other small furry beasts, who romped so
close to him that he thought they would be crushed
under the hooves of his horse. Orfeo dismounted
then, and walked along leading his horse by the bridle,
looking at the flowers and blooming trees.

There were strange shrubs and plants growing
here which he could give no name to, for he had never
seen their like before. One small tree in particular
caught his attention. This tree looked as if it had been
grafted with several different kinds of branches, although Sir Orfeo could not imagine what gardener
could have performed such work in the heart of the
forest.

And the tree presented a most strange appearance. Some of its branches were laden with white
or pink blossoms, which were suitable enough at this
season of the year, but others bore nothing but glossy
green leaves, and some were covered with golden
berries. Thus the tree looked as it might in spring,
summer, and autumn, all at the same time. When he

examined the berries more closely, he found that they were exactly like those of the wreath which had crowned his lady Etain when he first laid eyes on her.

Thinking *I shall take some of these back to her,* Sir Orfeo broke off a spray of the golden berries. But as he touched the tree, it vibrated oddly. When he pulled away the sprig, the whole tree shuddered as if something were moving beneath its roots, and the leaves rustled as if a high wind had suddenly sprung up.

While he stood there, looking first at the tree and then at the berries he held in his hand, a loud horn blast sounded deep in the forest. Although no other horns answered its shrill notes, the noise echoed and re-echoed in the wood. It was most uncomfortably loud and discordant. Orfeo knew, somehow, that this was one of the horns that he had hoped would never sound again in his land.

He stood in that place for some time, but no other sound came to his ears. In fact, the forest became all too quiet. There was no sign of the animals who had been so friendly, no stirring among the treetops or in the long grass. Troubled by all this, he tied the golden berries in his belt and mounted his horse again. He rode slowly back to his castle, looking out for his fellow knights on the way, but there was no one about.

Now as he rode up into the courtyard, wondering that no one appeared at the gate, Sir Amilon came running out to meet him and said, as he helped him

dismount, "Oh, my lord, you must come to your lady at once! She seems to have taken ill, or to have suffered a terrible shock, and is acting as if she had lost her wits."

"Where is she, and what has happened?" Orfeo asked.

"She is in her bedchamber," answered Sir Amilon, "but no one knows what is the matter. Her ladies say that she awoke from her noonday nap with a terrible, strangled scream, and began to weep and tear at her clothes and hair in such a frenzy of grief that they were horrified. They could not get her to speak to them, or to tell them what was afflicting her so. At last they had to send for help, and a group of serving men and ladies carried her home and put her to bed. Now she wants to flee, though no man knows what it is that frightens her so. She has not spoken a word anyone can understand, except to call out your name."

Sir Orfeo rushed to his lady's chamber. He stopped on the threshold for a moment, overcome with grief and horror when he saw Etain tossing on her bed like a bird trying to fight its way out of a net. Two of her ladies leaned over her on either side, vainly attempting to soothe her. Etain's face was swollen with tears and stained with her own blood, for she had been tearing at her shoulders and cheeks. Her hair and her clothes were in wild disarray.

As Orfeo stepped forward, he heard her wailing as

if her heart would break. But when he now stood before her, she suddenly stopped. From wild lamentations and ceaseless motion, she stiffened into a stillness like that of a marble statue, so suddenly that it was almost more frightening than her wild activity before. Now all that moved was her eyes as she turned her gaze on her husband and stared, with an expression of utter despair, at the branch he held in his hands.

The Invisible Host

rfeo knelt by her side and, putting the branch of golden berries on the coverlet, took her hands in his own and rubbed them gently. "Dearest love," he said, "tell me what is the matter and how I can be of help to you."

It was some time before Etain made any response. But he kept on speaking to her, and at last she turned her eyes to his face, sighed, and said, with tears streaming from her eyes, "Alas, my dear lord Orfeo, our love and our life together are now at an end."

"That cannot be," said Orfeo firmly. "Whatever has happened, my love for you shall know no end. You

must be calm, dear Etain, and remember the happiness
we have shared. All will yet be well.''

''You do not understand,'' said Etain, sobbing
bitterly. ''I well remember all that from which I am
loath to part. But I cannot stay with you any longer. I
must go, whatever you do now!''

''But why? What do you mean? What makes you
wish to leave me so?'' protested Orfeo.

''Oh,'' she cried, ''never have I wished to leave
you—but I must. I cannot stay here, no matter how I
long to.''

''But where will you go, dear one? Wherever you
wish to go, I shall go with you,'' Orfeo said.

''No mortal man may go where I must go,'' said
Etain. ''Alas, that ever we parted in the forest today!
But I shall tell you all I can of what happened. As I
slept there, under that oak tree, a terrible dream came
to me. Two young knights appeared before me. They
wore gleaming garments of white and silver and carried
spears of gold. They smiled, but their cold, glittering
eyes struck terror into my heart. They spoke curtly to
me, saying that I must come with them to speak to
their lord the king, whom they called Midir.''

''Midir!'' gasped an elderly woman who had been
helping Etain's attendants. ''May God save you!''
With a shudder, she pulled her cloak over her head and
blindly groped her way out of the room.

The other men and women in the room stared

47

after her, then exchanged puzzled glances. The name of Midir meant nothing to them.

Now Etain continued her story: "I told the two knights that I certainly would not go with them, and I felt much relieved when they turned abruptly and rode away. But in a short while a much larger troop of riders appeared. Both knights and ladies, all dazzlingly fair to look upon, came riding on milk-white horses with silver hooves, two by two. They surrounded me almost completely, taking their places in a circle around the oak tree, leaving a small gap through which the last few riders came. These were, first, the two knights I had seen before; then four others dressed in the same way; then, last, their king, who rode straight up to me.

"He was a tall, fair man, most handsome, yet his appearance filled me with deadly fear. His brightness so dazzled my eyes that I wished to look away, but I could not. His golden hair was crowned with a circlet of gleaming silver, and the silvery glance of his gray eyes seemed to dart into my very soul. His white shield was emblazoned with spiraling circles of silver and gold, glittering in the sunlight, and he carried a strange five-pointed spear in his hand.

"This king did not speak a word to me, but simply leaned down, gathered me up, and placed me before him on his horse. I did not dare to struggle, for he rode off as swiftly as the wind, and I was terrified. We seemed to be whirling up through the air, then downward again, through void and darkness. At last he stopped and bid me look around me. I was in an exceedingly strange land where everything glowed with a radiance that came not from the sky but, rather, from within every object the eye could see. Smooth fields ran down to sparkling streams, which burst into fountains, watering a multitude of gardens. The landscape was dotted with shining towers and castles.

"In the midst of this land was the king's own palace. It shone most brightly of all, for it was made of a sort of crystal which was no color at all and yet every color there is. Now the king set me down in the midst of the palace garden, and led me up to a tree covered with golden berries—berries that I knew right well. 'Lady,' he said, 'know that there are branches of this tree planted in the forest where you and your company have been roaming. They are there because you have been living in that land; for your life is bound to that of this tree. But some of those berries have now been rudely broken from their stem. For this reason, your days in the world of men are over: it is time for you to return and dwell with us here forever.'

"I wept and protested, begging him to have mercy, but he made no answer at all, except to pull me up on his horse again and bring me back to the oak tree in the forest. But when he had set me down once more, he spoke for the last time, saying, 'I shall send my riders for you here in this place tomorrow, just at noon. Do not try to escape us. If you are not waiting here for us, we shall find you, wherever you are, and it will be the worse for you and all those around you.' Then he vanished, and I awoke.''

When Etain had finished, she buried her face in her hands, and rocked back and forth in her grief. Sir Orfeo turned to the other ladies and asked, ''Did any of you see any part of such a vision, or note any trace of riders in the forest?''

''No, my lord,'' answered the ladies. They were plainly frightened by Etain's account, and many of them were weeping as bitterly as she was herself.

''It was only a dream, then,'' said Orfeo. ''Come, my dear, a dream is but a picture in the mind, nothing but fantasy.''

''This was no fantasy,'' Etain replied. ''It was true, as it is plain to see. The proof lies before us in the golden berries you have brought here.''

In vain, Orfeo tried to explain that this was only chance. But he did not feel sure of this himself, when he remembered what had happened when he picked the berries. At last he said, ''We shall take counsel then, and decide what is to be done.''

Now Sir Orfeo went into the state chambers with all his counselors, and they argued and talked of possible measures on into the night; but it was impossible to know what to do when they had so little

understanding of the meaning of Etain's vision.
Amilon finally suggested that they should speak to the
old woman who had fled when she heard the name of
Midir, to learn what she might be able to tell them.
When she had been brought to them, most unwilling-
ly, they found it difficult to persuade her to speak.
After Orfeo had begged her to tell what she could, she
looked around her tearfully and said in a low voice,
"Lord, if Midir has summoned your lady, there is
nothing you can do. You will never see her again."

"But who is Midir?" he asked.

"Some say he is a god," said the old woman, "and
some that he is king of Faerie. He rules a land, both
near and far, which some say is that of the dead."

"Tell me, then," said Sir Orfeo, "how I can best
keep him from taking my lady from me."

"You cannot," said she, and she closed her
mouth firmly and refused to answer any more questions.

At last the men decided that it would be best to
take Etain back to the oak tree at the forest, lest she
should risk unknown harm by staying away. They
would guard her with all their might. Each man swore
he would do all he could to see that no one laid hands
on her, and with this agreement they rose and went to
bed. In the morning they called for their weapons and
prepared as carefully as if they had been going to war.
Then, as midday approached, a procession of knights

in armor rode out toward the forest, with the lady Etain in their midst.

When they reached the great oak tree, Etain sat down in its shade, and Orfeo sat beside her, holding her hand in his. Forming a triple circle about them were sixty well-armed men, with their shields overlapping each other to make a solid wall of steel. It would have been hard indeed for any enemy to force his way through such a shield wall. Yet none of this comforted Etain, who shrank fearfully against her husband's shoulder.

As the sun reached its highest point in the heavens, a peal of hunting horns rang out in the forest, wild and shrill and discordant, as it had before the death of the steward Ganlin. At first the noise was far away, but it sounded again and again, and each time it grew closer. As the horns closed in on them, the knights drew their swords and stood braced for anything that might come.

Then the beat of many horses' hooves was heard, as if a mighty troop were bearing down upon them. Yet nothing could be seen. Suddenly the knights standing on guard felt a mysterious force, like a mighty wind, pushing them all over into an untidy heap. Then invisible arms held Sir Orfeo still in his place, while Etain was swept up into the air. Within a few seconds she had disappeared from their sight completely.

There was a final triumphant blast from a horn,

and then the noise retreated, as if the invisible host were rushing away. Horns sounded from farther and farther off, till at last the shrill noise died out in the distance. Orfeo still lay on the ground, helpless with grief. There was nothing his companions could do but urge him to return to his castle, and at last he did so.

As the group of knights returned that afternoon, the ladies ran out to meet them anxiously, looking for Etain among them. But she was not to be found, and they had but to look at the men's faces to see what had happened. They broke into wails of grief for their lost lady; sorrow descended on the land like a black cloud.

As for Sir Orfeo, he retreated into his chamber at once, and locked the door behind him. No one could persuade him to come out or to take food or drink, and he was not to be seen for the next three days.

Harping in the Forest

n the fourth day after the disappear-
ance of the lady Etain, Sir Orfeo came
out from his chamber, dressed in
somber mourning clothes. He called
all his knights to a special council
meeting. When they were gathered
in the great hall, he spoke to them and
said, "My friends, it is time I appointed a new steward.
To this office I name Sir Amilon. From this day
onward, it is my wish that he take my place at the head
of this realm, governing the land and its people on my
behalf. I ask you all to accept him, freely granting him
the honor and obedience that you owe to me."

No one objected to the lord's choice of a steward, but there was an uneasy stir at Sir Orfeo's suggestion that the steward was to rule in his place. Still, the council gave its approval and Sir Amilon duly became steward of the land.

"Now," said Sir Orfeo, "I wish you to know that since I have lost my wife, I intend to shun the company of others and live where I will never have to be reminded of her by the presence of other women. I shall leave my lands in Sir Amilon's care and go out into the wilderness alone. There I shall live from now on, with no company but that of the wild beasts. I know, however, that you will wish to arrange for the government of the realm after my time has passed. Therefore I ask you to meet together when such time has gone by that you think I must be dead, unless you hear sure tidings of my death sooner than you expect. When that time comes, hold a high council and choose yourselves a new lord."

"My good lord, you cannot mean this!" said Sir Amilon. "Be patient. In time, your grief will grow less, and you will marry again and furnish us with an heir."

"That I shall never do," said Sir Orfeo. "Unless Etain is returned to me, I shall live alone the rest of my life."

A great uproar arose as everyone protested Orfeo's decision. Some of the men wept, and others rushed up and fell on their knees before him, begging him to change his mind. But it was of no use. Orfeo brought the council to an end by simply walking out of the palace, carrying nothing but his harp. He strode through the streets of his town, past the astonished men and women, and on into the forest. His people wept and lamented behind him, but he did not look back.

There he stayed, wandering ever farther into the wilderness, in fair weather and foul. His fine clothes were soon tattered rags, his shoes so worn that he had to go barefoot. Instead of a comfortable bed with rich woven coverlets, the bare ground was his resting place, leaves and moss his only covering. When winter came and brought snow and icy winds, he had no place to take shelter except damp caverns, and no food to eat but the bark of trees and such roots as he could dig up with his hands.

Nor was his diet much better in the summertime: berries, grasses, and wild fruits were not what he had been accustomed to eat in his pleasant palace. He became so thin that it would have been shocking to see, if there had been anyone there to see it. His knights and ladies would scarcely have recognized his face, for his beard grew down to his waist and a rough tangle of hair all but hid his eyes and sunburned cheeks.

For more than ten long years Sir Orfeo lived in the

forest, with no company but that of the wild beasts, and no joy in the world except the music of his harp. He kept the harp hidden in a hollow tree most of the time, but when the sun was shining, and he did not need to spend every moment keeping warm or searching for food, he would bring it out and play so that all the wood resounded with his sweet, sad melody. He sang:

> Farewell to my palace, pleasures, and play;
> Welcome is wildwood and forest way:
> Sweet Etain's exile I wish to share.
> My royal robes and my rich array
> Are changed for mourning of solemn gray,
> My mantle of silk for a shirt of hair.
> I shall make my bed with beaver and bear,
> With badger and boar shall I lead my life,
> Dine on green grasses with deer and hare:
> Lost, lost, is lovely Etain, my wife.

Whenever he sang, wild creatures came and gathered around him. Hundreds of birds would flock to the nearby bushes to listen, while small, shy furry animals crept up through the grass and even the wildest and most dangerous beasts of the wilderness ceased their roaring and pressed close to hear the music of Orfeo's harp. Sometimes it seemed to him the very trees and stones moved closer when he played his harp, but he thought he must have imagined this. He did notice, though, that none of the wild animals ever tried to harm him. He lived among them as peacefully as if they had been the house cats and hunting dogs of his own castle; yet they kept their distance when he was not playing his harp.

Orfeo did find other company in the woods from time to time. At least, he sometimes caught sight of other creatures. But those who rode about him, deep in the forest, were not from the world of men and women at all. They were, rather, the figures he knew to have been involved in his loss of the lady Etain. If that had been the work of Faerie, then they were of that strange world. It was usually around noon on a warm, sunny day that he saw these groups—sometimes beautiful, but always alarming—riding by.

At times he saw the Wild Hunt, rushing by with shrill blasts on many hunting horns, with hounds running along beside the horses, adding their echoing barks to the general din. That these were no ordinary hunters was easy to see. For one thing, they never seemed to take any game, or even to be chasing the creatures of the forest. The animals were quite uncon- cerned by their passing: even the shy deer stood still and peered through the thickets at the passing hunt rather than running away in flight.

But the hunters did not look harmless. Orfeo was chilled to the spine to see them pass, for not only did one of them appear to be newly hanged, as he had earlier heard, but others were riding along easily despite missing limbs. One of them even rode without a head.

In striking contrast to this group—but in its way just as terrifying—was another troop of riders he sometimes saw. This was a great host of knights on milk-white horses, all dressed in the white and silver that Etain had described. There must have been many thousands in this host, all clad in glittering armor and carrying drawn swords. Their faces were solemn and grim, and their eyes stared straight ahead, with never a glance to either side. Bright banners fluttered from their spears as they went past, while the wood echoed with the thunder of many hooves. Yet there was never a bent blade of grass or a broken twig to show which way they had gone. Like the Wild Hunt, they passed, leaving no sign that they had ever been there.

A third group, which Orfeo saw at times, was made up of both knights and ladies. This troop did not ride by, but appeared—Orfeo had no idea how—here and there in the forest, sometimes in one place and sometimes in another one far away. He never found them in the same place twice. He would come upon them unexpectedly, where he had been quite sure there was no sign of any creature a few moments before. All at once he would hear a lively tune played on pipes and trumpets and drums, and there would be

a circle of dancers, whirling about. Yet he could never find out who played for their revels, for there were no musicians to be seen. When they had finished their dance, the knights and ladies would clap their hands and step back, and then vanish from his sight.

Sir Orfeo became so used to such odd comings and goings in the forest that he did not always stop to watch. But one day he suddenly saw yet another group, riding along a stream. This time there were only ladies in the band, some sixty of them. All of them had hawks or falcons perched on their wrists, as if they were hunting for wild fowl. He could tell from their shimmering garments and the silvery gleam of their horses' hooves that these riders also came from the strange world of Faerie, yet since he had never seen a Faerie host actually capture any game, he was curious to see whether this group would be an exception. Thus he followed behind the ladies, wondering what they would do next.

He found that like the huntsmen with their hounds they seemed to pay no attention to the game, although birds flew up around their heads in flocks. After a while they stopped where the stream widened into a quiet pool. There they dismounted, and leaving their horses to graze and drink the waters of the pool, they began to sing and dance together. Orfeo was standing quite close to the dancers, and as he watched them swirl about it occurred to him that one of the dancers looked very much like his lady Etain. He could not resist moving still closer, and soon he was able to see the dancer's face quite clearly. There was no question in his mind: this was Etain.

Now, as the dancers twisted and turned, he found himself face to face with his lady. At the same moment she saw him, and although he was so changed that no one else in the world could have recognized him, Etain knew him at once. She stopped absolutely still and caught her breath with a gasp. He would have rushed to her side, but she held out one hand as though to push him back, and put the other over her mouth in a gesture calling for silence. He could see a stream of tears running from her eyes.

The other ladies quickly noticed the odd behavior of their comrade, and formed a circle around her, completely hiding her from Orfeo's view. In a very few moments they were all mounted on their horses again, prepared to ride away. But Orfeo had no intention of letting his lady out of his sight. He picked up his harp, wrapped his tattered cloak around him, and ran after them as fast as he could. As they were riding along the banks of the stream, he managed to keep them in sight, and hopes of another glimpse of Etain gave him the strength to run as he never had before in all his life.

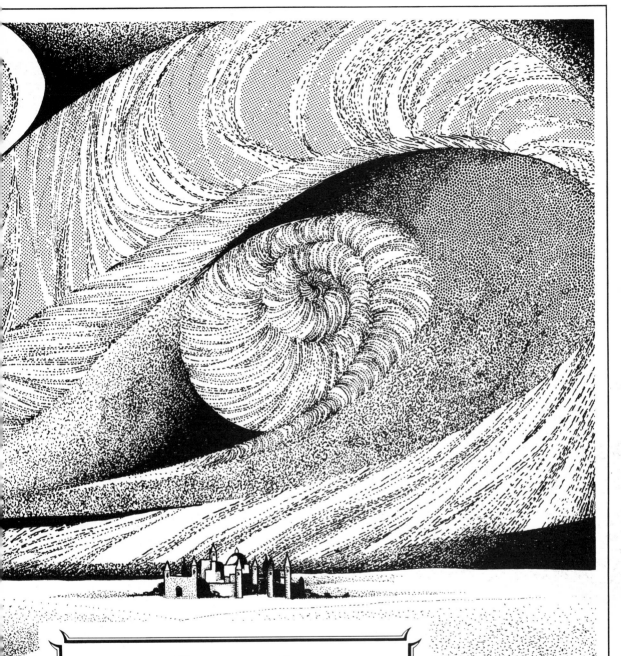

Beneath
the Crystal Cliff

t the end of the valley, the stream crossed a flat plain and flowed into a larger stream, one that could be called a river. On the opposite shore of this river towered a tall rock that gleamed in the afternoon light. Orfeo watched with amazement as the band of ladies rode straight across the river and vanished into the face of the rock. He hastened along behind them, and when he arrived at the bank of the river, he saw that the rock face was a crystal cliff, which caught and reflected the light. There was one dark spot in the center; this, he thought, must be the gap through which the riders had disappeared.

Sir Orfeo was determined to follow them. He looked for a shallow spot where the river could be easily crossed, but although the water was bright and clear, he could not see the bottom anywhere, nor did he find any sign of fish or plants in the water. Orfeo was hot and thirsty after his long run, and the clean, shining water looked most attractive. He leaned over the bank to dip in his hands for a cooling drink, but just at that moment a stray leaf fluttered into the water. As soon as it hit the surface it shriveled up and vanished. There was not so much as a ripple on the smooth, glassy surface of the water to show where it had been.

After this, the water did not look so appealing, and Orfeo saw that it might be very dangerous to try to cross this river. But he was not going to let it stand between him and his lady. His one best chance was to try to leap over the water. Tying his harp securely to a corner of his cloak, he stepped back some way to make a running start, then leapt up as hard as he could. He barely managed to make it across the river, and now found himself clinging to the jagged edges of the cliff, in great danger of falling back. As he struggled there, his dagger fell out of his belt. It struck the surface of the water and vanished into nothingness while he watched.

But at last Orfeo was able to pull himself onto the ledge that ran along the bank of the stream, and there he found, as he had thought he would, a cavelike opening into the crystal face of the cliff. Peering into this gap, he could see nothing but darkness. However, he knew the band of ladies must have gone this way, and he did not hesitate to plunge right into the darkness and grope his way forward. Orfeo could feel smooth walls on either side of him. He kept moving forward, following the walls as he went.

He wondered what he would do if the way branched and he had to make a choice, but, fortunately, this did not happen. In fact, it became clear that this tunnel was absolutely straight, always leading in a downward direction. He went on this way for a very long time without seeing a single glimmer of light or hearing any sound but his own echoing footsteps. When he had gone at least two miles, he began to feel quite uneasy about this path, wondering if it had an end. He tried not to think what he might find if it did come to an end.

At last Sir Orfeo saw a faint glimmer of light. He hastened more eagerly onward, and suddenly emerged from the tunnel, blinking, as his eyes were dazzled by light. There before him was a strange flat land, without any trace of hills or valleys, bathed in an eerie light. It seemed to come from within rather than from above, as Etain had said of the light on the land she had seen in her vision. His heart lifted, for he felt sure that here he would find his wife. Nor did he have to look hard to see what direction to take: in that flat land, the buildings that dotted the landscape were very plain to see.

One of them stood right at the center, and he knew at once that this must be the palace of the king called Midir. It was much higher than any other building to be seen, and far more impressive. The palace was surrounded by a wall of shining crystal, as bright as the cliff through which he had come. From this wall rose at least a hundred towers and pinnacles, and here and there he could see rooftops of gleaming gold. He went on toward this great palace, through pleasant gardens and past many murmuring fountains, until he reached a gate, which was firmly shut.

There was nothing to do but knock and hope that he would be admitted. For a while his knocking produced no result, but at last he heard a shuffling step and a porter appeared. This was a very aged man indeed. Orfeo thought he had never seen anyone so old. The porter's long beard was as white as snow, and he seemed barely able to move. He was clearly astonished to see Sir Orfeo at the gate. "What man may you be?" he asked. "You do not belong in this land."

"No," Orfeo agreed. "I am a wandering minstrel. We harpers go from one place to another, playing music for all who will hear. I have come to play before your lord, if he will admit me."

The porter looked at Orfeo's harp, and, although

he still looked very puzzled, he slowly unlocked the gate and pulled it back so that Orfeo could enter. Now as Sir Orfeo came within the wall, he saw servants going about their business, and men and women strolling around or taking their rest on benches along the inside of the wall. It would have been an ordinary scene, except that some of them were maimed and terrible to see: in fact, he saw there many of the wild huntsmen he had seen riding through the forest. In this serene courtyard, their appearance was more horrifying than ever.

The porter was waiting for Orfeo to follow him into the castle hall, so Sir Orfeo turned away from the dreadful sights that had greeted him. He was led into a splendid, bright hall, which was lit by a thousand gems set in the walls. He could see rubies and emeralds gleaming there, with a thousand other rare and precious stones. A throng of knights and ladies were seated on benches that ran all around the huge room. He had seen many of them before, too, but here they looked even more beautiful and terrifying than they had when he had glimpsed them in the forest.

At one end of the room, the king sat on a high throne. Orfeo hardly dared to look at him, for the glance of his brilliant eyes seemed to go right through him. Instead, he turned his gaze to the queen who sat on another throne by Midir's side. Orfeo stood rooted to the spot as he looked at her face, unable to believe

his eyes. It was his own lady Etain, dressed in royal garments and crowned with a circlet of shining gold. She was as lovely to look upon as she had ever been, but she was pale and thin, and her face was solemn and sad. She stared back at him with wide, frightened eyes. Etain's terror was plain to see, and just as she had done in the forest, she quickly gestured to him to keep silent.

It was clear that she did not wish anyone to know that he had recognized her, and equally clear that it was for his sake that she was afraid. He could hardly bear to see the tears that sprang to her eyes. But he obeyed her silent request, and looked away. Casting his eyes down toward the richly paved floor, he said, "If it please your majesty, I have come to sing for you."

The king now spoke in a stern voice, "What manner of man are you, who dare to come to my hall so boldly? I never sent for you, nor did any of my people bring you here."

"Lord," said Sir Orfeo, "I am a poor minstrel. It is our custom to seek out the homes of great lords so that we may offer them our music: we have no other way of earning our living but by the rewards we thus gain. Let me show you what I can give you."

He took up his harp, tuned it, and played a melody which charmed the ears of everyone in that hall. When he had finished, the king said, "Well done, minstrel. Play something more for us, for your music is most welcome.''

''We poor harpers must live by our music,'' said Orfeo. ''If I please you with my song, will you give me the reward I seek?''

''Whatever you wish, your reward shall be even greater,'' said the king.

Orfeo touched the harp again, and began to sing:

Merry it is while summer doth last
With sweet birds' song;
But now nears the winter's blast,
North winds blow strong.
Dark, oh, dark! This night is long!
And I, who suffer endless wrong,
Must sorrow and mourn and fast.

As he sang, everyone in the palace was drawn into the hall to listen, nor did anyone make a sound until the last note of the harp had died away. Then the king nodded, and said, ''Sir minstrel, you have earned the richest reward you can ask. Tell me what it is that you wish, and you shall have it at once, and more.''

''Lord king,'' Sir Orfeo answered, ''I ask you to give me that fair lady who sits by your side.''

Everyone gasped, and the king frowned in anger. ''Do not be absurd, minstrel,'' he said. ''I promised

you that you might have whatever you wished, but that certainly did not include my own queen. How dreadful a thing it would be to let her be given to a ragged beggar like you!''

''Sir,'' said Orfeo, ''it would be an even more terrible thing for such a lord as you to break his promise. I ask nothing in the world but that lady. Keep your word, and give me what I ask.''

King Midir sat and stared at the harper for some time. No one dared to break the silence. At last he said, ''Well, minstrel, I will keep my promise, but under one condition. You must pick out the lady you want from among a crowd of others, where you shall not know her by her crown or royal robes.''

''I will gladly agree to that,'' said Sir Orfeo.

The ladies then retired from the room, and the king and his knights sat there smiling distantly. At last the door opened again, and in came a band of a hundred ladies, all dressed exactly alike. All of them were pale and fair, with grave faces and long, lovely golden hair. But Orfeo showed no sign of confusion. He walked into the center of the group, took the lady of his choice by the hand, and said, ''This is the lady I claim, lord.''

The lady smiled up at him, for she was indeed his own Etain. And now the king could hardly go back on his promise a second time. After another brief silence, he said, "Then I must let her go with you. But what do you intend to do with her?"

"I shall take her away from here," Orfeo replied.

"You will not find that easy," said the king. "No mortal man has ever found a way to leave my realm."

"I found a way to come here, lord, and I shall find a way to return," said Orfeo.

"I see," said the king. "Well, I said I would give you more than you asked, and I shall keep that promise, too. You shall have a horse on which to carry the lady. The horse will take you to the borders of my realm and bring you safely over the river that surrounds it. But when you find yourself on the other side of the water, you must dismount and send back the horse to me. He will find his way by himself."

Sir Orfeo agreed to do this. Now he knelt and humbly thanked the king, who waved him away impatiently. "I hope, minstrel," said he, "that you have some safe place to take your prize. Poor lady, she has not been used to the sort of life you lead."

"I had such a place once, lord king," Orfeo answered. "If I no longer do, I shall have to see what can be found."

"Then begone," said the king, "before I change my mind. You will find your horse waiting by the gate."

The Harmonious
Kingdom

ing Midir's white horse carried Orfeo and Etain safely out of his country, but they were glad enough to send it back: they had no desire to retain any part of the realm of Faerie. Now, however, Orfeo's problem was to decide whether he dared to take his wife back to his own land. It had been many long years since he had left his palace. He had no way of knowing whether Amilon was still serving as his steward, or how matters stood in that land. Perhaps his own return would be most unwelcome to those who now enjoyed his power and riches.

He pondered these questions in his mind as he and Etain made their way through the wilderness, hand in hand. His companion felt none of his fears: joyfully content to be with her beloved Orfeo again, she said that she would gladly live with him in a cave, or anywhere else he might see fit. She was quite at home in the forest, where she sang merrily as she helped to gather food for their simple meals. But the day came when they reached the borders of the land called Tracience.

There in the forest Orfeo found the very same cottage where he had stayed with Amilon long ago, when they were returning from Camelot. Stopping out of sight of the cottage, Orfeo told Etain that he thought it would be best for him to approach the woodman alone. He could not be sure it would still be the same woodman, but in any case he had reason to be careful. For one thing, he realized that he did not look like a suitable companion for a lovely lady, and it was possible that some armed knight would try to take her away from him. He therefore left Etain behind, hidden in a grove of trees, while he went to find the woodman and to seek shelter for the night.

When he went alone up to the cottage, he quickly recognized his old friend the woodman, who looked up from his work in the garden as Orfeo approached. It was hardly surprising that he did not look as welcoming as he had before, for what he saw was not a handsome knight but a shabby, ragged, dirty wild man of the wood: a figure many would have fled from in terror. The woodman, however, merely wished Orfeo good day, politely enough, and waited to see what he had to say.

"Good forester," said Sir Orfeo, "can you give shelter and protection to a lady in distress?"

"What sort of lady might that be?" asked the woodman clearly astounded.

"A noble and gentle lady is in my care," said Sir Orfeo. "She is in need of rest and shelter. If you will be so kind as to welcome her, I shall leave her here while I go to search for her kin."

The forester marveled that any lady at all could have fallen into the company of such a wild man, but Orfeo simply said he could answer no questions. Finally the woodman agreed that the stranger might leave the lady there. Orfeo now went back and brought Etain out, with her face hidden in her hood. The woodman received her kindly, thinking it understandable such a fine lady might not wish to be seen.

When she had been led to the best seat by the fireside, the good man busied himself and soon produced ample food for both of his guests, which they received gratefully. Orfeo would very much have liked to question his host about the land and its rulers, but he did not dare. He feared that whatever he might say would betray the fact that he knew more than a wild man of the forest should.

As the three oddly assorted people settled down to sleep in the forest cottage that night, two of them, then, suffered from unsatisfied curiosity. The third, Etain, slept peacefully, without fear of the future, for she trusted her husband completely. In the morning, Orfeo rose early and took his leave of the other two, telling them that he would surely return by nightfall that day, whatever tidings he might have. Then he turned away and strode through the forest toward the meadows and farmlands of his own realm.

As Sir Orfeo once more walked through the streets of his native city, men and women stopped in their tracks to stare at the wild man from the forest with a harp hanging over his shoulder. Minstrels had always been common in this land, but never had one been seen in such filthy rags, with a beard that hung almost to his knees and a tangled mat of hair hiding his face. There was much whispering and pointing, while children either laughed aloud or ran in terror from the unfamiliar sight. But Orfeo paid no attention, as far as could be seen. He walked straight on, along the road that led to the castle gate.

Not far from the palace, he came upon a group of knights who had been strolling along together. Suddenly he found himself face to face with his steward, Sir Amilon. Amilon, of course, had no idea who this wild man was. "Sir knight," cried Orfeo, falling on his knees, "have mercy on a poor minstrel! I am a harper from a faraway land. Help me in my distress!"

Sir Amilon gazed down at him in some surprise, but quickly said, "Come with me, minstrel; I will share my meal with you. Every harper is welcome in this place."

He extended a hand to Sir Orfeo and led him into the hall of the castle, where the table was set for the steward's dinner. There he placed Orfeo in a place of honor, surrounded by knights and noble ladies, who, if they minded sharing their bread with a ragged beggar, did not say so or in any way act other than with the greatest courtesy. Amilon saw that Orfeo was served with all the best dishes before he took his own place in the steward's high seat. As his own meal was now served, trumpets blew and drums sounded, while harpers and pipers struck up their tunes.

Melodious music poured through the hall, as it had in the happy days long ago, before Etain vanished from the land. Orfeo sat quietly, eating sparingly of the many dishes offered to him and listening to the music. When everyone was finished and the musicians were resting and refreshing themselves, Orfeo brought out his own harp, and when he had tuned it he struck up a lovely melody and sang:

> *The law that turns the starry spheres*
> *In place as they advance*
> *Makes music, which each planet hears,*
> *To guide the rhythmic dance.*

This law is heavenly harmony,
Whose rules the skies obey:
Who turns with tides the surging sea
And tames its restless sway.

The seasons change at her command
As day gives way to night,
For harmony's controlling hand
Allows both dark and light.

O men, look up: learn from above
To end your bitter strife!
Let faithful friendship, loyal love,
Thus harmonize your life.

No one stirred until he had finished. Then Sir Amilon stared very hard at the harper and said, "Minstrel, may I see your harp?"

Without a word, Orfeo passed it to him. The steward turned it over in his hands and looked at it carefully, with a set, frowning face. Finally he spoke again. "Minstrel," he said, "where did you get this harp? Pray tell me exactly how it came to fall into your hands."

"Sir," answered Orfeo, "some years ago I was wandering in a distant country, far away from here—in a deep wilderness, where there was no sign of the dwellings of men. There I came across the body of a man who had been killed by fierce wild beasts—lions, or wolves perhaps. The wolves had been gnawing at his body, and what was left of it was terribly torn. This harp lay by his side. I buried his remains as best I could, but took his harp, for I could see that it was a good one.''

Sir Amilon covered his face with his cloak and cried out sharply. ''Alas,'' he said, ''that ever I lived to hear such dreadful tidings! That was my lord Sir Orfeo, for I know his harp as well as I know my own right hand. Alas for this land, that has lost so good a lord, and alas for my dear friend, who has met so frightful a death!'' He bent over the table in his grief, weeping bitterly.

Knights and ladies jumped up from their benches and went to him, trying to offer him comfort: but they were all weeping themselves. It was some time before anyone in the room was able to speak calmly again. The ragged harper looked at the scene of sorrow all around him and said wonderingly, ''Then was this lord so well liked in your land, steward?''

''No man was ever better beloved,'' said Sir Amilon. ''I do not know how we shall bear our loss.''

''If I were Sir Orfeo,'' the harper then said, in a rather different tone of voice, ''and had returned to this land after many years of hardship, I should certainly be most gladdened to find my steward so faithful. It is not every man who has such good friends as this.''

Something about his voice now caused all the men and women in the room to turn and look carefully at him. Sir Amilon slowly rose from his seat, with his eyes fixed on the ragged figure of the minstrel. "My lord!" he gasped, and all at once he pushed over the table in front of him as he bounded to Orfeo's feet and knelt down before him. Now rejoicing broke out in the hall as the people all recognized their lord and flocked about to look at him more closely.

When the noise and confusion had died down, Orfeo said, "Yes, I have returned, and this time I shall stay here for good, since I find such a welcome among you. And I have not returned alone: I have brought my wife, the lady Etain, won back from Faerie by the power of the harp."

Everyone wept for sheer joy, while the castle bells rang out in peal after peal, bringing the glad tidings to the folk of the land. Now Orfeo let his men lead him away to be shaved and washed and dressed in fine new clothes.

It was thus a very different figure who arrived at the woodman's cottage that evening. The ragged wild man who had left the lady in the forester's care that morning had disappeared forever. With the lord came a large troop of knights, who greeted their lady with the utmost joy and escorted her back through the town, to the tune of all sorts of merry melodies and hearty cheers on all sides.

Back in their pleasant palace, Sir Orfeo and his
lady lived in joy and harmony for many happy years,
rejoicing in each other's company and in the friendship
of all their people. But most of all they valued the
friendship of Sir Amilon, who kept the title of high
steward for the rest of his life, and was his lord's chief
helper in watching over the welfare of the land.

A Note on the Sources

From Harmony, from heavenly Harmony
This universal frame began. . . .
—"A SONG FOR SAINT CECILIA'S DAY, 1687"

Dryden's lines on harmony voice a thought that was commonplace by the seventeenth century: music, in the medieval scheme of things, had long been a symbol of order of various kinds, including matrimonial and social concord. Thus the ancient myth of Orpheus, as told by Ovid and Virgil, had a special appeal for the Middle Ages. However, the most

96

influential version of the period was the brief account in *The Consolation of Philosophy* of Boethius. In another well-known passage of that work, Boethius spoke of the Love that ordains concord in the universe, reflected both in the movement of the heavenly spheres and in the ideals of orderly human society, specifically government by law, marriage, and friendship. These two Boethian passages seem to have been fused in the imaginations of at least two poets. Robert Henryson, writing in Scotland in the late fifteenth century, depicts Orpheus learning his musical skills directly from the music of the spheres.

The other, the anonymous English poet of the fourteenth-century *Sir Orfeo,* was even more daring, for he gave the tragic old story what might be termed a Boethian ending: the supremely harmonious harping of Orfeo not only wins him back his beloved wife, but also plays an important role in the ordering, and regaining, of his kingdom. Readers today are likely to overlook the significance of the musical theme here, and thus to find this version a soft, sentimentalized "fairy tale"—which is a pity, for it is an interesting work in its own terms. Nor is it a "fairy tale" in the condescending sense sometimes used today. It is true that the classical land of the dead is transformed into a land of "Faerie," but this beautiful yet sinister land, drawn from Celtic myth and folklore, has nothing to do with the genteel fairyland of Victorian children's literature.

The *Orfeo* poet, then, reshaped his tale to bring it in line with the interests and understanding of his audience—a task all tellers of tales must try to accomplish—making use of Celtic materials as well as classical sources. In my retelling I have added more from both source groups, taking a hint, for example, from Virgil's association of Eurydice with the forest nymphs, while bringing other aspects of the story closer to the lines of the parallel Old Irish *Wooing of Etain.* As the poet moved his story into an English context, just familiar enough to his readers, I have, for similar reasons, located it in the Britain of the romances. I like to think that my greatest predecessor as a writer of romances, Chrétien de Troyes, would have approved, for he did much the same thing when he combined the Celtic tale of the Lady of the Fountain with the classical Grateful Lion motif, and placed the resulting story, *Yvain,* in Arthur's Britain.

But my expansion is, perhaps, not so much a reshaping as a gloss on the text, a more explicit statement of the poem's meaning. Thus my "false steward" exists to illuminate the poet's "faithful steward," my unorthodox subjection of the heroine to an "Accused Queen" gambit to underline the nature of the human relationship involved. In the process, I have, as usual, borrowed from a multitude of sources beyond the primary and most obvious ones: even Orfeo's "songs" are borrowed from medieval sources. One is adapted from a meter of Boethius, one from Henryson's *Orpheus and Eurydice,* and the others from Middle English lyrics. And, finally, I am also indebted to the host of fellow scholars who helped to shape my understanding of the material, not least my former colleague Howard Nimchinsky, whose Columbia University dissertation on *Sir Orfeo* I read with pleasure and profit.

ABOUT THE AUTHOR

As a medieval scholar, Constance Hieatt has especially enjoyed retelling Arthurian legends for young readers. THE MINSTREL KNIGHT is a companion volume to her earlier books: *Sir Gawain and the Green Knight, The Knight of the Lion, The Knight of the Cart, The Joy of the Court, The Sword and the Grail,* and *The Castles of Ladies.* Mrs. Hieatt is a specialist in Old and Middle English, and the author of several texts, translations, and scholarly commentaries. She has taught at Queensborough Community College and at St. John's University in New York, and is now Professor of English at the University of Western Ontario in London, Ontario.

Mrs. Hieatt was born in Boston, Massachusetts, and attended Smith College. She received her A.B. and A.M. degrees from Hunter College, and her Ph.D. from Yale University. She and her husband, who is also a professor of English, spend much of their time in England, where their home is part of a remodeled manor house in a village near Oxford.

ABOUT THE ARTIST

James Barkley's illustrations for THE MINSTREL KNIGHT, like those of many earlier illustrators of Arthurian tales, are set in a period much later than that of the historic Arthur. And like the poets who retold these ancient legends, the artist has incorporated elements from the work of his predecessors. Botticelli's lovely "Primavera" was the model for the Lady Etain, and details of costume, architecture, and armor are derived from Flemish and Italian paintings of the Renaissance.

James Barkley is well known as a commercial artist, illustrator, and painter. His work has been honored by the Society of Illustrators, the Art Directors' Club, and the American Institute of Graphic Arts. He has traveled to Alaska to do a series of paintings on our national parks, and designed and painted the Mount McKinley air-mail stamp for the National Park Centennial. Born in New York City, Mr. Barkley is a graduate of the School of Visual Arts, and has taught at the Parsons School of Design. With his wife and two children he now lives in Pleasantville, New York.

J398.2--H
Hieatt
The minstrel knight

DISCARD

Rockingham Public Library

Harrisonburg, Virginia

1. Books may be kept two weeks and may be renewed twice for the same period, unless reserved.

2. A fine is charged for each day a book is not returned according to the above rule. No book will be issued to any person incurring such a fine until it has been paid.

3. All injuries to books beyond reasonable wear and all losses shall be made good to the satisfaction of the Librarian.

4. Each borrower is held responsible for all books charged on his card and for all fines accruing on the same.